FOLK TALES FROM AFRICA:
THE GIRL WHO MARRIED A LION

Also by Alexander McCall Smith

The No. 1 Ladies' Detective Agency Series

The Sunday Philosophy Club Series

Short Stories

FOLK TALES
FROM AFRICA:

The Girl Who Married A Lion

ALEXANDER
McCALL SMITH

CANONGATE

Edinburgh · New York · Melbourne

This edition first published in 2005 by
Canongate Books Ltd, 14 High Street,
Edinburgh, EH1 1TE

1

The following stories first published in
The Girl Who Married a Lion in 2004
'A Bad Way to Treat Friends'
'Tremendously Clever Tricks Are Played, But to Limited Effect'
Copyright © Alexander McCall Smith 2004

Other stories first published in *Children of Wax* in 1989 by
Canongate Books Ltd
Copyright © Alexander McCall Smith 1989

Illustrations copyright © Naomi Holwill, 2005

The moral rights of the author and illustrator have been asserted

British Library Cataloguing-in-Publication Data
A catalogue record for this book is available on
request from the British Library

Typeset in Fournier by
Sharon McTeir, Creative Publishing Services,
Oldhamstocks, Dunbar, Scotland
Printed and bound in Great Britain by
Clays Ltd, St Ives plc

ISBN 1 84195 729 1

www.canongate.net

For Finola O'Sullivan

CONTENTS

THE TALES

Introduction

How can a girl possibly marry a lion? Surely the lion would eat her, and that would be the end of that. And how could a girl drown, but be brought back to life by crocodiles? And as for talking leopards and clever baboons – impossible!

Of course it's all impossible, but then these are folk stories and such stories, wherever they come from, are all about things like this. Nobody thinks they are true, but what they tell us about how people think and behave is often really very true indeed. So it doesn't matter if leopards cannot talk, because the story may not be about leopards at all, but about people.

Folk stories are stories which are passed down from person to person. At first such stories are not written down, but are remembered by people, who tell them to their children and grandchildren. And then these children and grandchildren remember them and tell them to their own children. And that's how the memory of these stories lasts and lasts.

The stories in this book are from two countries in Africa – Botswana and Zimbabwe. I collected many of them quite some time ago by going round and asking people to tell me stories that they remembered. Some of the people I asked were old people – others were children at school. Everybody was very kind and helpful. They loved telling me their stories. Then, later on, I asked a friend to collect some stories from Botswana and write them down for me. I added these stories to this collection.

The stories are often funny, but sometimes they are sad – just like life itself. They all tell us something about things like courage and selfishness. They show us that it's not very clever to trick others, that you should be kind to your friends and to people who are weaker than you are, and so on. I think that I agree with most of the things that they tell us, and I suspect that you will too!

There is another thing that they show you, and that is that there are some very exciting and beautiful things in Africa. I hope that even if you have not thought very much about Africa before, these stories might make you interested in that beautiful place. And at the end of the day, the stories tell you that people in Africa are just like the rest of us – they have the same hopes, the same worries, and they find the same things funny.

The money from this book, by the way, is going to help people in one African country, Zimbabwe. There is a hospital there which needs help to buy medicines for sick people, including sick children. When you bought this book, you helped the doctors and nurses there to help others. And that could be a story in itself, couldn't it?

But enough of this. There are hares and baboons and snakes and the rest waiting to share their adventures with you. Some of them are good, but some are bad. So be careful! (But have fun, of course.)

Alexander McCall Smith
Edinburgh 2005

I

A Bad Way To Treat Friends

It used to be that Leopard, Goat, Guinea Fowl and Wild Cat were all good friends. They lived together in the same place, near some hills that came out of the plains, and where there was good water and cool places to sleep.

Goat had some very fine children, of which she was justly proud. They were strong and healthy and they could stand on their back legs and eat the leaves from the shrubs that other animals could not reach. They were very clever children, too, and knew a lot about the world, which made other children envious. Leopard's children were not very strong. They could not run as fast as leopard

children normally run, and their coats were dull and matted.

When Leopard saw Goat's children playing in the grass, her heart was filled with hatred for them. These children made her own children look so thin and weak that she wished that they could be got rid of. In that way her own children would be the healthiest and strongest children in that place. But how was she to get Goat to go away for long enough for her to deal with Goat's children? The idea came to her that she would ask Goat to go and look for a new dress for her, as she had been invited – or so she would say – to a party to be held by her cousins.

Goat agreed to Leopard's request, and she went off to the other side of the river to look for a fine new dress for her friend, Leopard. She left her children behind, telling them not to wander away but to stay within sight of Leopard, who would look after them. These strong children, who were also very obedient, agreed to do what their mother had asked them. All the time, Leopard was watching this, watching, watching.

Once Goat had gone, Leopard crouched down and began to stalk Goat's children through the long grass. The poor children, not knowing the danger that was now so close to them, were full of happiness. Then, in an instant, Leopard was upon them. She seized them and carried them back to her place by the scruff of their necks. The children thought that this must be a game, as Leopard was their mother's friend, and they continued to laugh and smile even as they were dragged along.

Once she had captured all the children, Leopard tied up their mouths and wrapped them in leaves. Now they were bundles ready to take off to the party, where Leopard and her cousins would eat them. Unknown to Leopard, though, Guinea Fowl and Wild Cat had returned from a journey, and they watched in dismay as they saw what Leopard was doing. They were saddened by the thought that Goat's happy children would no longer be jumping up and down in the grass and singing their goat songs that they all so liked to hear. They could

not believe that Leopard would be wicked enough to do such a thing, but now they saw it all before their very eyes.

Shortly afterwards, Goat returned from the other side of the river, bearing a fine new dress which she had bought for Leopard. Leopard was very pleased with this, as she was a vain person who liked to wear fine dresses and admire her reflection in the water.

While Leopard was busy trying on her new dress, Guinea Fowl and Wild Cat crept round to the place where the parcels were stored and they took the leaves off Goat's children.

"You must go and hide," they said to the children. "Make sure that Leopard doesn't see you, though, for she is very wicked."

Goat's children, shocked by what had happened to them, went off into the bushes, stifling their tears as they did so. Guinea Fowl and Wild Cat did not go with them, as they had business to do. Seeing Leopard's children nearby, they went over to them and very quickly overpowered them. It was not difficult to do that, as Leopard's children were weak and sickly. Then they wrapped them in leaves – the very leaves which only a short time ago had been wrapped around Goat's children.

It was now time for everybody to set off to the party. Leopard, who was pleased with herself in her new dress, did not bother to find out where her children were and had no idea that they were inside the parcels which she was carrying. So when Guinea Fowl and Wild Cat asked her what was in these parcels, she replied only that there was good meat for them to have at the party.

When they arrived at the party, Leopard told her cousins that they should put the parcels into the pot unopened. She did not want Goat, who was there, to see that her children were being put into the pot. Guinea Fowl, though, realised the danger that they were in, and she whispered to Goat and Wild Cat that they should all run away before the parcels were taken out of the pot.

Later when Leopard took out the parcels and opened them, she saw that her own children were inside and had been cooked. This made her cry out in anger and run back to their place by the hills, so that she might catch Goat and her children and punish them. But they had left by the time she got there, and that is why even to this day we see leopards searching for goats.

2

Hare Fools
The Baboons

A clever hare realized that the lion was always welcomed by the other animals. This was not because the other animals liked the lion; it was because they were all afraid of him. If the lion came to another animal's house then it was wisest to give him a lot of food. If the hare ever went to another animal's house, then he was more likely to be told to go away.

"This is unfair," the hare said to himself. "I could do with the food that everybody gives the lion."

Calling on the lion one day, the hare told him that he was very skilled at getting lice out of lion tails.

"I can tell that you have lice in your tail," the hare said. "Can you not feel them itching?"

The lion thought for a moment. Now that the hare had mentioned it, he was sure that he could feel an itching in his tail.

"Remove the lice from my tail," he roared at the hare. "Do it right now!"

The hare smiled and said that he would set to work

13

straight away. Quickly he went to the back of the lion and laid out his great tail on the floor. Then, taking a handful of long nails from a bag that he had with him, he hammered a nail through the lion's tail and into the floor.

The lion called out in pain and told the hare to be more careful.

"I'm sorry," said the hare. "These are very large lice. They are angry that I am catching them and that is why they are biting you so hard. You'll just have to put up with it until I'm finished."

The lion grunted and lay still while the hare pretended to search for another louse. When he was ready, he took out another long nail and quickly hammered it through the lion's tail. This time the lion roared even louder.

"That was a very large louse," the hare said. "But don't worry, I have taken him off."

"How many more are there?" asked the lion, his eyes watering with pain.

"Three," replied the hare. "And all of them seem to be very large."

Each of the last three lice seemed more and more painful to the lion, and he howled more loudly each time the hare drove another nail into the floor. Finally the hare was finished and he came round to face the

lion. Looking him directly in the eye – in a way in which no other animal would dare – the hare calmly walked over to the place where the lion kept his food and began to help himself.

The lion was so astonished at the hare's cheek that at first he did nothing. Then, roaring with rage, he tried to leap to his feet, only to be wrenched back painfully by his nailed tail.

"Release me at once!" he roared at the hare. But the other just laughed, and ate more of the lion's food. Then, when he had eaten enough, he sauntered over to another part of the lion's house and found a large knife. The lion watched him suspiciously, and tried to swipe at him with his claws, but he could barely move now and it was easy for Hare to get round him. Deftly waving his knife, Hare split the lion's skin from one end to the other and pushed him out of it. Once he was out of his skin, Lion was just a weak jelly, with no claws and no teeth. Hare pushed him aside and straight away began to free the tail of the now empty lion skin. Once he had finished this task, he slipped into the skin and bounded out of the house.

The baboons were frightened when they saw what they thought was the lion. Carefully they laid out a great deal of food so that the lion would eat it and not bother them. Inside the lion skin, the hare smiled to himself and cheerfully began to eat the food. When he had finished, he lay out on the ground and relaxed his lion claws. It would be pleasant to sleep in comfort in that place and wait for the baboons to bring him more food in the evening.

The next day, since the hare was eating so much food, the baboons had to travel far afield to find food for their store caves. The hare stayed put, and when his hosts had gone he slipped out of the lion skin to play with the baboon children. They enjoyed their games, with the hare chasing them in circles and the baboon children trying to catch him by his ears. Just before the baboon parents came back, however, Hare got into the lion skin and was a lion again. The baboons had found a great

deal of food but he managed to eat up most
of it and told them that they would have to
go out again the next day to find more.

That night, the baboon children told their
parents that the lion was not really a
lion but a hare dressed up as one. The
parents did not believe them, and warned
them not to say such things. One baboon,
though, was suspicious, and he decided to hide the
next day and see what really happened when the
adult baboons had gone in search of food.

Of course the hare slipped out of his skin again
and enjoyed more games with the baboon children.
This was watched from a bush by the hidden baboon,
whose eyes glowed with anger as he saw the deception
which he and his friends had suffered at the hands of
the wily hare.

"That lion is not a lion," the baboon whispered to the
others when they returned. "The children were telling
the truth – he is really a hare."

"I see," said the leader of the baboons. "We shall
have to drive him away."

Taking a large stick, the head baboon went up to
the sleeping lion and hit him firmly on the nose. This
woke up the hare, who felt the sharp blow to his nose
and howled with pain.

"That is not the sort of noise that a lion makes," said the baboon. And with that he beat the hare again, putting all his strength into the strokes. Had the lion been a real lion, of course, that would have been the end of that baboon, but it was really only a hare and a frightened hare at that. Leaping out of the skin, he ran off into the bush, to be pursued by the angry shouts of the baboons.

The baboons took the empty lion skin back to the real lion, who was still just a weak pink thing without his claws and mane. He was grateful to be able to get into his skin, and promised that he would not trouble those baboons again. This made the baboons happy, and they decided that although they still felt angry at the way the hare had tricked them out of food, some good had come of it and they would forgive him after all.

3
Sister Of
Bones

A family who lived in a dry place had two daughters. It would have been better for them to have had more girls, as there was a lot of work for women to do there. In the mornings there was cooking to do for the breakfast. Then, as the sun rose higher, there was maize to pound into powder and the yard to sweep. There were also other people's children to look after.

The hardest work, though, was the collecting of water. In the rain season there was a spring nearby which gave good, clear water for everybody to drink, but when it was dry, as it often was, the only place where water could be found was in a river a long way off. To reach the river, people had to leave in the early morning and they would only be back at midday.

It was not easy carrying calabashes of water back from the river. The sun was hot in the sky above and a dry wind came from the hills. Often the only companions along the path would be the lizards scurrying off in the dust or the cicadas screeching in the bush.

For many years it had been the task of the first girl to go to the river for water. The second girl was not nearly as strong as her sister. Her arms were thin and it was difficult for her to walk long distances. When she was asked to carry anything, the load felt twice as heavy to her as it did to her stronger sister. For this reason, most of her work was at home, plucking chickens or doing other things which required little strength.

The mother and father of that family had spoken to many people about what was wrong with that girl. They had taken her to a witchdoctor, who had pinched her thin arms and rubbed a thick paste on them.

"That will make them strong," he had said.

They kept the paste on the arms until it had all rubbed off, but the second girl's arms remained thin.

"She will always be weak," her mother said to her father. "We must accept that she is a weak girl."

The second girl felt sad that she was not as strong as the first girl, but she did not complain. There was plenty of work even for weak girls in that dry place.

The first girl always fetched her water from the same spot. There was a pool in the river there, and a path

that led straight down to the edge of the water. It was a place where animals came to drink, and each morning she could tell from the footprints which animals had been there before her. She could tell the marks of the leopards – who always drank at night – and the tiny marks of the duiker, who came shyly down to the river just as the sun was rising.

Every day the first girl would dip her calabashes into the pool and draw out the cool river water. Then, with the calabashes full, she would dip her hand into the pool and take up a few mouthfuls of water before she began the long journey home.

One day she felt very tired when she arrived at the river's edge. It had been especially hot that day, and it seemed to her that all her strength had been drained by the long walk. As she leaned forward to fill her calabashes, the first girl felt her head spinning around. She tried to stand up again, but she could not and slowly she tumbled forward into the water.

The river was deep and the first girl could not swim. For a few moments she struggled to get back to the edge of the pool, but there was a current in the water and it tugged at her limbs. Soon she was out in the middle of the river and it was there that she sank, with nobody to see her or to hear her last cry. Only some timid monkeys in a tree by the edge of the river saw the first girl disappear. For a few minutes they stared at the ripples in the water where she had been and then they turned away and were gone.

When the first girl had not returned by sunset, the father knew that something had happened to her. There was nothing he could do during the night, as there were lions nearby, but the next morning all the men went out to search for the first girl. They followed her footprints, which were clear on the ground, and traced her steps to the edge of the water. When they saw that the steps did not come back from the river's side, they cried out in sorrow, for they knew now what had happened to the first girl.

There was great sadness in that home. Everybody had loved the first girl, who had always smiled and been happy in her work. The second girl slept alone in her hut, sadly staring at the emptiness where the first girl had had her sleeping mat.

Now there was no choice but for the second girl to fetch the water each day. She set off before dawn the next morning, her heart full of sadness, wondering whether she would ever be able to carry the calabashes all the way back from the river. It was only after stopping many times that she managed her task, and when she had returned she felt as if she would never be able to walk again. Of course she knew that when the next morning came she would have to set out again, and that this task would have to be performed every day until the rains came again.

For three days the second girl fetched water from the river, and each day it became harder and harder. On the fourth day, when she reached the edge of the river she dropped her calabashes on the ground and sang the song that she had made for her sister. In this song, she told how her sister had come to the river and fallen in.

In that river there were many crocodiles. They would lie out on sandbanks or float just below the surface of the water, carefully watching the animals that came to the river to drink. When they heard this song, the crocodiles slipped into the river and quietly swam closer so that they could hear the words more clearly. It was a sad song and even the crocodiles felt sorry for her.

After the song was finished, the second girl sat at the river's edge, waiting for the return of what little strength she had. The crocodiles, though, swam away into the middle of the river, to the place where the first girl had drowned. Then, diving down to the bottom of the river, they gathered the bones of the first girl and took them to a special rock they knew on the other side of the river. There they put the bones together again and made them into a girl again. They carried this girl back to where the second girl was sitting and left her there.

When the second girl saw that her sister had come back, she cried out in joy and kissed her.

"I shall carry your water," the first girl said, "I am stronger."

The first girl carried the calabashes almost all the way back, but just before the village she had to stop and allow the second girl to carry them in.

"The crocodiles will not want me to leave the river now," she said. "I must go back."

From that day onwards, whenever the second girl reached the river the first girl would be there waiting for her. After the calabashes had been filled, she would put them on her head and shoulders and carry them

back for the second girl, singing all the while and telling her sister stories of what happened in the river. The second girl was happy to have her sister back and was happy too that everybody now thought that she was strong. She tried to tell her mother and father that she was helped by the first girl, but they cried out in anger that her sister was dead.

"She is not," the second girl said quietly. "Come with me to the river tomorrow and you shall see."

The parents went with the second girl the next day and were happy when they saw the first girl waiting by the bank. In gratitude to the crocodiles, the father put out some meat on a rock where he knew that crocodiles liked to sit. The crocodiles smelled the meat and swallowed it quickly in their great jaws. Then they went back to some other rocks and watched the family in all its happiness.

4

Beware Of Friends You Cannot Trust

Hyena was miserable. It was some time since he had eaten, and there was no food to be seen anywhere. He sat by the side of the road and tried to remember his last meal, but all he could think of was the pain that was gnawing away at his stomach.

As Hyena sat in misery, Jackal walked past. He was never miserable, as he always had enough to eat. He looked at hyena and asked him why he was so downcast.

"It is because I have had no food for days," Hyena howled. "Other animals are fat and sleek, but I am just bones. It might be better if I were to die now, rather than to wait."

"Well your troubles are over, Uncle," said Jackal. "It happens that I know a very good place for food."

"Will you show it to me?" asked Hyena. "I only want a little."

"I will do that with pleasure," said Jackal, preening himself as he spoke. "All you have to do is follow me."

The two friends made their way to a place which Jackal knew. It was a place where men lived, and it had a stock pen around which the men had built a high fence.

"This is the place," said Jackal. "That pen is full of sheep and goats. We can eat as much as we like."

"But what about the fence?" asked Hyena. "It is far too high for us to jump over."

Jackal smirked. "I have a way in," he said confidently.

"There is a hole in that fence. It is only a small hole, but we shall be able to squeeze through it."

Hyena followed Jackal to the place where the hole was. As Jackal had said, it was not a big hole, but they both just managed to get through and found themselves standing in the animal pen. And Jackal had been right. There were many sheep and goats standing about, peering at the two unwelcome visitors, waiting to be eaten.

"Do not eat the goats," Jackal whispered. "They make a great noise and will wake the men. Eat only the sheep."

The two friends then chased some sheep into a corner.

"You eat the fat one," said Jackal. "I will eat the small one."

Hyena though that this was most generous of Jackal, as had he been in Jackal's position he would undoubtedly have chosen to eat the fat sheep.

The sheep tasted good. Hyena ate and ate until he had eventually finished even the bones and skin of the fat sheep. Jackal finished his sheep more quickly, as it was much smaller.

Then they prepared to leave. As he stood up, Hyena felt his belly sag beneath him. It had been a very long time since he had had such a large amount to eat and his skin was stretched thin to accommodate all the delicious meat.

"I will just take one bite out of a goat," Jackal announced. "Goat meat is very delicious and it would help the rest of my meal go down."

No sooner had he said this, than he pounced on a goat and took a bite out of its leg. The goat cried out and made a terrible bleating noise. This awoke the dogs who were sleeping near the huts. They barked furiously and in due course awoke the men.

"We shall have to leave quickly,"

31

said Jackal, darting for the hole by which they had entered.

Jackal slipped out of the hole without difficulty, but when it came to Hyena's turn he was so round from eating the fat sheep that he could not get through. He struggled and wriggled, but it was no good. Soon the people were upon him, beating him with their knob-kerries and shouting angry words at him. By the time he managed to escape, he was covered with dreadful bruises.

Hyena went off to a quiet place and wept. He had now forgotten the delicious meal which he had enjoyed and all that remained was the burning pain from the blows which the people had inflicted on him. Hyena wept many tears. Some were for the shame of what had been done to him; others were over friends who could not be trusted.

5
Brave Hunter

There were many brave hunters in those days, but there was only one of them who liked danger. Other hunters faced up to danger when they went hunting, but did not go out of their way to find it. This man was different: it would have been easy for him to hunt in the flat land, where there were wide skies and light, but he chose instead to go into dark and thick forests. There he met leopards, snakes and some creatures that were half animal, half person and very dangerous. None of these creatures frightened this brave hunter, who would come home and tell people of what he had seen. As they listened to his stories, everybody knew that this was a hunter whose heart was stronger and harder than any other's in that part of the country.

This hunter married a girl who was soon expecting his child. All the people who knew her were looking forward to the day when the child was due to be born, as they knew that it would be a most unusual child. If it was a boy, then it would be as brave as its father; if it was a girl, then it would be more beautiful than any other children. The woman knew this too, and she faced each day with the smile of one who realizes that she is worthy of her brave husband.

The hunter was overjoyed when his wife gave birth to a strong boy. He heard the child crying lustily from the birthing hut and he gave a leap of delight when he recognized the cry as the cry of a male child.

"A small hunter is born," he said to his friends.

And they nodded and said: "He will be very brave – just like you."

So proud was the father of his child that he decided that the naming ceremony would be one which would be remembered by people for many years. For this reason, he announced to all his friends that at the ceremony he would take the life of a leopard cub, as a sacrifice for the future of his young son.

The hunter's friends were astonished at this claim. They all knew that to take a leopard cub from its mother was the most dangerous thing that any man could do. At the same time, they realized that if anybody could do such a thing, then it would be this brave hunter.

The hunter chose the darkest and most dangerous forest for the place where he would find the leopard cub for sacrifice. He showed no fear as he wandered into this forest, and paid no attention to the whispering sounds and the cracking of twigs which were all about him. Soon he found a place that smelled strongly of leopard and there, in a small clearing, were two leopard cubs, sleeping up against one another for comfort and warmth. Before the cubs could run away, the hunter swooped upon them and carried the little creatures out of the forest. It was a very brave thing to do, but a thing that only a man with a heart as hard as his would have done.

The people who saw him return with the two baby leopards were filled with excitement. They talked of nothing else and made special beer for the brave hunter to drink while he told them of how he had found the cubs in the darkest part of the darkest forest.

When the leopard mother returned, she called her children, but received no answer. She searched through the forest for them, looking under all the trees and bushes and into all the secret forest places which leopards like to lie in. The more she called, the emptier the forest seemed, and slowly she came to understand that her cubs had been taken away. When she saw the tracks that the hunter had made as he left the forest, she knew in her heart that a terrible thing had happened to her children and she cried deep tears for the cubs she had loved so much.

Her eyes full of these tears, the leopard mother followed the tracks back towards the village. As she came closer to the place where the people lived, she slowly changed herself into a beautiful woman. By the time she reached the hunter's house she was one of the most beautiful women who had ever walked past that place.

When the hunter looked out of his hut and saw a beautiful woman standing in front of it, he called out in his brave voice:

"What are you doing in front of my house?"

The leopard mother looked into the darkness of the hut and said:

"I am a stranger and I have no place to sleep tonight. I am frightened that I shall be in danger because I am not nearly as brave as you are."

These words pleased the hunter, who shouted out to her that she could spend that night in his hut. The leopard mother said that she was very grateful to him for his kindness and she entered the hut and lay down upon the floor.

As darkness fell, the leopard mother asked the hunter what he was going to be doing the next day.

"It is the naming ceremony of my young son," he said proudly. "I shall be sacrificing two baby leopards to mark the special occasion. My son shall have the skins to sleep upon when he is ready to leave his mother."

The leopard mother looked up at the brave hunter and begged him to spare the lives of the two cubs.

"They are only leopards," she said. "But please be generous to them and let them live. Think how sad their mother will be."

The hunter laughed at the suggestion which came from this beautiful woman and replied that it would be impossible for him to change his mind. He had already

39

announced to the whole village that the cubs would be sacrificed and they would not think him brave if he changed his mind.

On hearing this, the leopard mother wept bitterly, but the hunter just watched as the beautiful woman sobbed on his floor. When she continued to weep, he lay back on his bed and told her that she should go outside and only come back when her crying had finished.

"Why weep for two leopards?" he asked. "They are not worth weeping over."

As he spoke, he suddenly saw that the beautiful woman on his floor was changing into a leopard. He tried to rise to his feet, but he was not quick enough. Before he could reach for his spear, the leopard mother was upon him, her sharp claws uncurled, her sleek ears swept back in anger. The brave hunter screamed, but nobody heard him.

* * *

The next morning the people waited outside his hut for the naming ceremony to begin and wondered why no sounds came from within. They could not see, of course, the leopard mother playing with her cubs in the forest, nor hear them singing their leopard songs in the darkness.

6

Stone Hare

It was a time when there was a great shortage of water. Throughout the country the waterholes had dried up, leaving only parched expanses of baked mud. Only one waterhole remained, and in that there was very little water.

The lion was so concerned about the problem that he called the animals together to discuss it.

"The only thing we can do is to take turns," he said. "If we each have only one drink a day, the waterhole will last until the rains come."

The animals all nodded at the wisdom of this suggestion and they agreed that this is what they would have to do. Even the hare agreed.

As the days passed, the system which the lion had suggested worked well. The shyer creatures would go to the waterhole early in the morning, drink a few sips of water, and then move away. As the morning wore

on, the other animals would come to the water's edge, drink just enough to keep them going for a day, and then go back to their search. The lion himself, who had a large belly which needed a great deal of water, took only a few mouthfuls and then walked away.

Hare, though, began to wonder why he was bothering to keep the promise he had made. Eventually one evening he went to the waterhole for a second visit. There was nobody about and he was able to plunge into the water and drink to his heart's delight. Then, when his thirst was quenched, he swam about in the remaining water, washing all the dust and dirt out of his fur.

When he got out, Hare looked back and saw that the water was badly muddied from where he had been cavorting. This worried him, as he knew that when the lion came for his drink the next day he would be very angry. Hare thought for a moment, and then he had an idea of how he would deal with this problem.

Picking up some mud in his paws, he quietly made his way to the place where he knew the hyena would sleep at night. Then, creeping up to the hyena, he smeared the mud all over the sleeping creature's legs. As he did so, he smiled with pleasure at the thought of his cleverness, realizing what would happen to the hyena the following day.

44

As Hare had imagined, Lion was furious when he was told that the water remaining in the hole had been stolen and muddied. He went round each of the animals and asked them if they knew who could have done such a treacherous thing. When Hare was asked, he responded quickly.

"I saw the hyena do it," he said. "I saw him last night – drinking the water and then swimming in it."

"Do you have any proof?" asked Lion.

"Look at his legs," Hare replied simply. "You will find your proof there."

Lion lost no time in seeking out the hyena. When he saw the mud on his legs, he roared in anger and asked Hyena why he had behaved in so selfish a manner.

"I do not understand what you are saying," the hyena replied.

This answer served only to enrage Lion further. With another roar, he bounded over to Hyena and killed him with one swipe. Hyena fell to the ground and was immediately divided into four pieces by Lion. Then Lion called the other animals to assist him in carrying Hyena to a place where they would be able to cook him for a feast. Hare was given a heavy piece and as he carried it along he sang under his

breath a song which told all about a clever hare who had fooled a stupid lion.

One of the other animals heard snatches of this song and asked Hare what it was about. Hare replied with a lie, but continued to sing about the doings of the clever hare, who was no longer thirsty and had clean fur.

Unfortunately for Hare, Lion's acute hearing enabled him to hear the words of the song. Lion dropped the piece of Hyena that he was carrying and began to chase Hare, warning him that he was about to join Hyena at the feast – but not as a guest!

Hare ran ahead of Lion but soon found himself trapped by a deep ravine. He had no way of escaping other than by turning himself into a smooth stone, which he did.

Lion stopped at the edge of the ravine and looked about him in puzzlement. He roared once or twice to see if he could frighten Hare into giving away his hiding place, but he did not succeed. Angry at the way in which he had been outwitted by this tricky creature, he picked up the smooth stone that lay at his feet and hurled it across to the other side of the ravine.

Hare sailed through the air, landing softly in the thick grass that grew on the other side of the ravine. Then, almost immediately, he changed himself back into a hare and called out in mockery to the lion.

Lion was angrier that ever before, but he was unable to do anything about his anger. The more that Lion roared, the more did Hare laugh and call out how clever he had been.

Lion realized – too late – that there were some tricky people who could never be trusted, and that Hare was one of them.

7
A Tree
To Sing To

This happened in a time of famine. For months there had been no rain and the sky was empty of clouds. People prayed for rain and used powerful magic to bring on the heavy purple clouds that would save the land, but all this was to no avail. The cattle became thinner and thinner as they nibbled at the last shreds of vegetation. Then, when these disappeared, there was nothing left but the dust and the cattle began to die.

But there was one man who was eating. This man, Sibanda, had found a tree which grew by the dusty bed of an empty river. It had been his shelter after a long walk in search of food and he had sat underneath it to rest before he continued on his way home. It was in a lonely place, and so Sibanda sang to make himself feel braver. Because he was hungry, the first words that came into his mind were about food, and so he sang:

49

I must have food. Oh, give me food!
Please give me food!

Sibanda sang these lines only once or twice when he heard a sound in the leaves above him. Thinking it might be a snake – for mambas like to hide in such trees – he leapt to his feet and gazed into the branches of the tree.

At first the poor man thought that his eyes were deceiving him. Perhaps I've been out in the fierce sun too long, he said to himself. Perhaps it is making me dream. But when he looked again, he saw that it was no dream. The tree was beginning to shower him with food. He lifted up his hands and caught the food that came down to him. It was real and it tasted very good. Never before had he tasted such food, and he had soon eaten it all up.

That evening, Sibanda sat at his fireside and watched his wife preparing the small amount of food that would have to feed the whole family. There was very little to eat, and he knew that all the children would be going to bed hungry that night.

"Here," said his wife. "Take your share."

Sibanda shook his head and passed the food on to his youngest child.

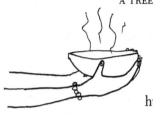

"My children must eat," he said. "I shall go hungry."

Of course he was not really hungry. In fact, he had eaten so much of the food that the tree had given him that he could hardly move.

When his wife saw what her husband was doing, she was filled with admiration for him. Here is a truly noble husband, she thought. Here is a man who will not eat when his family is hungry.

The following day Sibanda made his way to the dry river bed and again found the tree that had provided him with food. I shall sing to it again, he decided. I shall eat again today.

Standing underneath the tree, Sibanda raised his head and sang loudly into the wide branches above him. This time he chose different words:

> They gobble down all the food at home:
> They won't leave any for me.

When the tree heard this sorrowful song, it moved its branches as if it were weeping. Sibanda watched the movement and then, to his delight, he saw food come showering down. Quickly he gathered it all up

51

and stuffed it into his mouth. Then he sat down, rubbing his swollen stomach, and went to sleep. He was filled with a great happiness and in his dreams he saw more and more food stretching out before him. They were the dreams of a well-fed man.

At home that evening, Sibanda once again declined the offer of food which his wife made.

"I have told you," he said. "I cannot eat until all my children are fat once more. I prefer to starve."

Sibanda's wife was astonished at her husband's goodness. I always thought him an ordinary man, she reflected. Now I know that the father of my children is a great man.

And so it continued for many days. Each morning Sibanda would sneak off to his food tree and sing to it about the greediness of his wife and family. And the tree, feeling sorry for him, would move its boughs, although there was no wind, and it would let down all sorts of delicious food. Then, when he could eat no more, Sibanda would return to his home and would refuse to eat. Like a man suffering much because he can

smell food but not touch it, he would watch his family take their miserable portion of thin soup, refusing himself to take his share.

It is possible that this might have gone on for months, had it not been for the curiosity of one of Sibanda's daughters. This girl, who had watched her father getting fatter and fatter, began to wonder how it was that a man could grow fat if he never ate. In times of drought it was usual for everyone to become thinner – indeed many feared that they might die. Yet her father, who ate nothing at all, was now the fattest man in the village.

This girl decided to follow her father. As he sneaked away one morning, she was watching him from behind a tree. Quietly, so as not to attract his attention, she followed him along the path that he took towards the river bed. When he reached the food tree, she hid herself behind a rock.

Quite unaware that one of his daughters was behind him, Sibanda reached the tree and began to sing to it:

My family eats like hungry dogs –
I wait at the side like a timid cat.

As usual, the tree disgorged its food, and the astonished girl watched her father eating with the speed of a man who has not eaten for many weeks. Then, when he went to sleep beneath the tree, 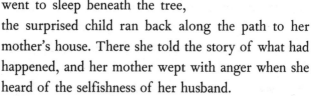 the surprised child ran back along the path to her mother's house. There she told the story of what had happened, and her mother wept with anger when she heard of the selfishness of her husband.

The next day, when Sibanda made his secret way to the river bed, he was followed by the whole family. He did not know that they were following him, for they moved silently, like thin dogs. But when he stood beneath the tree, the woman and her children ran out shouting. Assembling all her children beneath the branches of the tree, she sang out to the trunk and the leaves:

> A selfish man stands here:
> He eats while his family grows thin.

When it heard this, the tree gave a great shudder. For a few seconds it seemed as if it would tear itself out by its roots, but after a while it calmed down and began to shed food for the hungry family.

"You see!" shouted the embarrassed man. "This tree has food for all of us."

Eagerly he bent down to pick up some food, but when he put it into his mouth he spat it out quickly. He tried some more, but had to do the same thing again, for everything that the tree gave him tasted bitter in his mouth. The food that the tree gave to the woman and her children was as sweet as ever.

8

A Blind Man
Catches A Bird

A young man married a woman whose brother was blind. The young man was eager to get to know his new brother-in-law and so he asked him if he would like to go hunting with him.

"I cannot see," the blind man said. "But you can help me see when we are out hunting together. We can go."

The young man led the blind man off into the bush. At first they followed a path that he knew and it was easy for the blind man to tag on behind the other. After a while, though, they went off into thicker bush, where the trees grew closely together and there were many places for the animals to hide. The blind man now held on to the arm of his sighted brother-in-law and told him many things about the sounds that they heard around them. Because he had no sight, he had a great ability to interpret the noises made by animals in the bush.

"There are warthogs around," he would say, "I can hear their noises over there."

Or: "That bird is preparing to fly. Listen to the sound of its wings unfolding."

To the brother-in-law, these sounds were meaningless, and he was most impressed at the blind man's ability to understand the bush although it must have been for him one great darkness.

They walked on for several hours, until they reached a place where they could set their traps. The blind man followed the other's advice, and put his trap in a place where birds might come for water. The other man put his trap a short distance away, taking care to disguise it so that no bird would know that it was there. He did not bother to disguise the blind man's trap, as it was hot and he was eager to get home to his new wife. The blind man thought that he had disguised his trap, but he did not see that he had failed to do so and any bird could tell that there was a trap there.

They returned to their hunting place the next day. The blind man was excited at the prospect of having caught something, and the young man had to tell him to keep quiet, or he would scare all the animals away. Even before they reached the traps, the blind man was able to tell that they had caught something.

"I can hear birds," he said. "There are birds in the traps."

When he reached his trap, the young man saw that he had caught a small bird. He took it out of the trap and put it in a pouch that he had brought with him. Then the two of them walked towards the blind man's trap.

"There is a bird in it," he said to the blind man. "You have caught a bird too."

As he spoke, he felt himself filling with jealousy. The blind man's bird was marvellously coloured, as if it had flown through a rainbow and been stained by the colours. The feathers from a bird such as that would make a fine present for his new wife, but the blind man had a wife too, and she would also want the feathers.

The young man bent down and took the blind man's bird from the trap. Then, quickly substituting his own bird, he passed it to the blind man and put the coloured bird into his own pouch.

"Here is your bird," he said to the blind man. "You may put it in your pouch."

The blind man reached out for the bird and took it. He felt it for a moment, his fingers passing over the wings and the breast. Then, without saying anything, he put the bird into his pouch and they began the trip home.

On their way home, the two men stopped to rest under a broad tree. As they sat there, they talked about many things. The young man was impressed with the wisdom of the blind man, who knew a great deal, although he could see nothing at all.

"Why do people fight with one another?" he asked the blind man. It was a question which had always troubled him and he wondered if the blind man could give him an answer.

The blind man said nothing for a few moments, but it was clear to the young man that he was thinking. Then the blind man raised his head, and it seemed to the young man as if the unseeing eyes were staring right into his soul. Quietly he gave his answer.

"Men fight because they do to each other what you have just done to me."

The words shocked the young man and made him ashamed. He tried to think of a response, but none came. Rising to his feet, he fetched his pouch, took out the brightly coloured bird and gave it back to the blind man.

The blind man took the bird, felt over it with his fingers, and smiled.

"Do you have any other questions for me?" he asked.

"Yes," said the young man. "How do men become friends after they have fought?"

The blind man smiled again.

"They do what you have just done," he said. "That's how they become friends again."

9
Hare Fools Lion – Again

A woman who used to go out to cut grass for thatching once came across a place where there was a great deal of grass. There had been good rains there, and the soil was rich and nourishing. Where the rains had fallen, the grass had grown higher than any other grass she had seen, and now it waved golden brown in the wind.

The woman was overjoyed at the sight of so much thatching grass and she immediately began to cut it down with her sickle. She worked at this task all day, pausing only to wipe her forehead of the beads of moisture that sprang from the hard work she was doing. From the side of the field, a hare was watching her, thinking what a good woman she was to do all this hard work while other people were sitting about under the trees and telling long stories about the hard work that they used to do a long time ago.

Toward the end of the afternoon, when all the heat had gone out of the sun, the woman stacked up the grass she had cut and loaded it onto her back. She was a strong woman, but even for her the weight of this load was almost more than she could manage. She was determined, though, that she would carry all this grass back to her husband, and so she staggered off down the path that led back towards her house.

The woman had only walked for a short distance when she felt that she would have to put her load down.

"If I don't rest," she said to herself, "my back will break."

After a short time, she again loaded the bundle of grass onto her back and began to walk again down the winding path. It was a path surrounded by dense bush, and she knew that it was a place where it was dangerous to stop too long. She was unwilling to linger long in that place, but soon she had to put her bundle down again. When she tried to load it onto her back, however,

she found that she just did not have the strength to do this.

"If only somebody would help me!" she called out in her distress. "If some strong person would help me carry this burden I should let him marry my daughter."

As she finished speaking there was a sound from the bush beside the path and out of it there came a large lion. He was the most powerful lion that the woman had ever seen, and she wailed in fright at the sight of his great shoulders and the shock of golden mane that framed his face.

"You need the help of a lion," the lion said to her. "Load that grass on my back and I shall carry it back to your house."

The woman was seized by fear, but she managed to get the bundle onto the back of the lion and together they walked down the path, the woman in front, leading the way, the lion behind, his lion breath hot against the bare skin of the woman's legs.

When the woman's husband saw his wife coming down the path, followed by a lion, he let out a great shout. All his friends, woken up by this cry, leapt to their feet and ran towards the fence of tree trunks, beating drums and shouting threats at the lion. The lion saw all these excited men, and although he was strong and brave, he decided to run away before they could throw

spears into his hide. As he ran, the grass fell off his back and was quickly scraped up into a bundle by the woman.

Many days passed after this strange event and the woman forgot all about the lion – and the promise she had made to him. When her husband suggested that they should all make a journey to see his uncle and his uncle's children, the woman readily agreed. Together with her husband and her daughter, she set off along the path that led to the uncle's house, not thinking of the fact that this path ran right past a place that was very much liked by large lions.

And indeed, there he was, waiting for them in the middle of the path, his great mane bristling, his strong shoulder muscles rippling like the surface of water in a breeze.

"So this is the daughter you promised me," the lion said. "She is very beautiful and I look forward to marrying her."

The husband looked in consternation at his wife, who merely lowered her gaze to the ground and told him that what the lion said was quite true. The girl, who had never seen a lion before, wept at the thought that she would have to marry such a frightening creature.

In some thick grass at the edge of the path, the hare sat watching the difficult situation that was now developing.

"Please! Please!" he shouted, as he bounded out onto the path. "Some help is needed!"

The lion looked at the hare and asked him why this help was needed.

"There are some rocks nearby," said the hare. "These rocks are about to fall. If they fall they will crush the crops that I have spent so much time growing. Please help me."

The lion was a bit unwilling to help such a small creature, but when he saw that the others were happy to do so, he grudgingly agreed. Pleased at their willingness to help, Hare led them through a field to a

place where there were great rocks of granite, balancing on one another, as often happens in that part of the country.

"You hold there," he said to the lion. "Lean against the rock with all your might."

The hare then positioned the three others underneath a rock, telling them to push against it with all their strength. Then he stood back and looked at the people supporting the balancing rocks.

"I have a very good idea," he said after a few moments. "If I get poles to hold up the rocks, this will be much less strain on your arms."

The lion and the people all agreed that this was a good idea, and so the hare went up to the man and said:

"You must go to a place nearby and look for a pole called 'Go for good and never come back.' Take your wife with you."

Then the hare walked up to the daughter and said to her:

"You must go to a place

68

nearby and look for a pole called 'Also go for good.'"

Then he stood back and watched while the three people went off in search of these poles. After a while, he called out to the lion that he was going to find out what had happened to the people.

"They are taking a very long time to find these poles," he said. "Please wait here while I go to find them."

The lion waited patiently under the rock. After several hours the others had still not returned and the next morning, when there was still no sign of any of them, he remembered the names of the poles. He was angry at being tricked and the people heard his roars from many miles away. They were safely in their houses, however, celebrating with the daughter her luck at being saved from such a frightening husband.

10

Strange Animal

There were many people to tell that boy what to do. There was his mother and his father, his grandfather, and his older brother. And there was also an aunt, who was always saying: "Do this. Do that." Every day this aunt would shout at him, and make a great noise that would frighten the birds.

The boy did not like his aunt. Sometimes he thought that he might go to some man to buy some medicine to put into her food to make her quiet, but of course he never did this. In spite of all his aunt's shouting and ordering about, the boy always obeyed her, as his father said he must.

"She has nothing to do but shout at you," the boy's father explained. "It keeps her happy."

"When I'm a big man I'll come and shout in her ear," the boy said. It was good to think about that.

There was a place that the aunt knew where a lot of fruit grew. It was a place which was quite far away, and the boy did not like going there. Near this place there were caves and the boy had heard that a strange animal lived in these caves. One of his friends had seen this strange animal and had warned people about going near that place.

But the aunt insisted on sending the boy to pick fruit there, and so he went, his heart a cold stone of fear inside him. He found the trees and began to pick the fruit, but a little later he heard the sound of something in the bush beside him. He stopped his task and stood near the tree in case the strange animal should be coming.

Out of the bush came the strange animal. It was just as his friend had described it and the boy was very frightened. Quickly he took out the drum which he had brought with him and began to beat it. The strange animal stopped, looked at the boy in surprise, and began to dance.

All day the boy played the drum, keeping the strange animal dancing. As long as he played the drum, he knew that there was nothing that the strange animal could do to harm him. At last, when night came, the strange animal stopped dancing and disappeared back into the bush. The boy knew that it had gone back to its cave and so he was able to walk home safely. When he reached home, though, his aunt had prepared her shouting.

"Where is all the fruit?" she shouted. Thinking that he had eaten it, she then began to beat him until the boy was able to run away from her and hide in his own hut.

The boy told his father the next day of the real reason why he had been unable to bring back fruit from the tree. He explained that there had been a strange animal there and that he had had to play his drum to keep the animal dancing. The father listened and told the story to the aunt, who scoffed at the boy.

"There are no strange animals at that place," she said. "You must be making all this up."

But the father believed the boy and said that the next day they would all go to the fruit place with him. The aunt thought that this was a waste of time, but she was not going to miss any chance of shouting, and so she came too.

When the family reached the tree there was no strange animal. The aunt began to pick fruit from the tree and stuff it into her mouth. Calling to the boy to give her his drum, she hung it on the branch of a tree in a place where he would not be able to get at it easily.

"You must pick fruit," she shouted to the

boy. "You must not play a drum in idleness."

The boy obeyed his aunt, but all the time he was listening for any sounds to come from the bush. He knew that sooner or later the strange animal would appear and that they would then all be in danger.

When the strange animal did come, it went straight to the boy's father and mother and quickly ate them up. Then the aunt tried to run away, but the strange animal ran after her and ate her too. While this was happening, the boy had the time to reach up for his drum from the branch of the fruit tree. Quickly he began to play this drum, which made the strange animal stop looking for people to eat and begin to dance.

As the boy played his drum faster and faster, the strange animal danced more and more quickly. Eventually the boy played so fast that the animal had to spit out the father and the mother. The boy was very pleased with this and began to play more slowly. At this, the strange animal's dancing became slower.

"You must play your drum fast again," the boy's father said. "Then the strange animal will have to spit out your aunt."

"Do I have to?" the boy asked, disappointed that he would not be allowed to

leave the aunt in the stomach of the strange animal.

"Yes," the boy's father said sternly. "You must."

Reluctantly, the boy again began to play the drum and the strange animal began to dance more quickly. After a few minutes it was dancing so quickly that it had to spit out the aunt. Then darkness came and the strange animal went back to its cave.

The aunt was very quiet during the journey back home. The next day she was quiet as well, and she never shouted at the boy again. Being swallowed by a strange animal had taught the aunt not to waste her time shouting; now, all that she wanted to do was to sit quietly in the sun.

The boy was very happy.

11

The Sad Story Of Tortoise And Snail

Tortoise and snail had been boys together and loved each other with a deep love. When either was away, the other was unable to sleep, but would lie awake, wondering when his friend would return.

Although as boys they had done everything together, their work as adults had been different. Tortoise had become a farmer, and had done nothing but grow crops; Snail, by contrast, had become a trader, and had many trading posts in all parts of the country.

Although Snail was happy in his work as a trader, and was always able to buy all the food that he needed, he longed to do what Tortoise did. When he saw Tortoise surveying his fields of ripening crops, he thought of the pleasure that must come from growing such fine food. There was no such pleasure in trading, where the only satisfaction was in making more and more money. Snail knew that this was not a satisfaction that would last forever, and so he went to Tortoise and spoke to him about his dream of becoming a farmer.

"If you give me some grain," he said to his friend, "then I shall be able to plant it in a small field that I have."

Tortoise was suspicious of Snail's request. He wondered why Snail wished to grow grain when he was rich enough to buy all the grain he could ever need. Could it be that Snail was trying to prove that he was cleverer than he? If that was so, it was a bad way to treat a friend and was not a request that he would be prepared to meet.

"I shall give you some corn to plant," he said to Snail. "Come back tomorrow and it will be ready for you."

Snail left Tortoise's house, happy that his plan to be a farmer seemed to be going so well. What he did not know, though, was that the moment he had left, Tortoise had taken a handful of corn and had put it into boiling water. There he left it until it was thoroughly boiled. Tortoise knew that in this state it would never germinate and Snail's field would grow nothing but weeds.

Snail planted his seeds when the first rains arrived. There were good rains that year, and in Tortoise's fields the crops grew tall and strong. Other people, too, had good crops, except for Snail, who spent his time cutting back weeds and examining the ground to see when the corn would grow. Tortoise said nothing about the failure of Snail's crop, although in private he was laughing. When Snail told him that next year he would try a new piece of land, Tortoise just nodded.

"I shall give you some good seeds," he said. "They will surely grow next year."

Snail planted the new seeds given to him by Tortoise. The rains were heavy again that year and there was much growth throughout the country, but in Snail's fields only weeds grew. Tortoise was sympathetic and made suggestions about how Snail might improve his farming. Snail, however, was now suspicious of the seed he had been given and when, the following year, Tortoise again gave him corn seed, he took it to hare. Hare looked at the seed and shook his head.

"This seed has been boiled," he pronounced. "It is good only for eating – here, try it."

Snail took one of the corn seeds and put it in his mouth. The seed had all the softness of boiled corn and the taste of his friend's deception was bitter in his mouth. Snail decided that he must have his revenge on Tortoise. Going to see his mother, he asked her if she could pretend to be dead. Then he went to Tortoise and told him of his misfortune, asking him to help him to bury his mother. Tortoise was quick to console him, and told him how sad it must be to lose a mother.

Snails bury their mothers in special places, and it was to one of these places that they carried what Tortoise thought was the body of Snail's mother. In fact, the body was nothing but a banana stem wrapped up in leaves, and the tears that Snail wept were not real tears.

Later, Snail asked Tortoise to come and pray with him at the grave, which was in front of a small bush. The two animals said their prayers and then, to Tortoise's surprise, they saw money falling in front of them.

"It is from my mother," Snail said. "If you pray at the grave of your mother, the mother will give you money."

Tortoise believed this. He had not seen Snail's mother hiding in the bush, and he had not heard her chuckles as she threw the money out before them. Snail's words remained in his mind for the rest of the day, and by evening he had made his plan.

The next morning Tortoise arrived at his mother's house, looking very sad.

"Why are you so sad?" his mother

asked. "Has something terrible happened to you?"

Tortoise shook his head. Then he looked at his mother and spoke angrily.

"Why are you still alive?" he asked. "Do you expect me to die before you?"

Tortoise's mother was surprised by this, but she answered calmly.

"I do not think I should die yet," she said. "There is no need."

Tortoise became angrier. "But are you not older than Snail's mother, who has already died?" he shouted. "Do you expect to live forever?"

"Not forever," Tortoise's mother answered. "I want to live only until I have eaten all the food I was meant to eat."

When he heard this answer, Tortoise stormed off. A few hours later he was back, carrying with him twenty baskets of food and twenty buckets of water. He put this burden down in front of his mother and told her to eat and drink, as this was about as much food and water as she was due by nature to consume.

"But I'm not hungry," his mother said. "So you must go away, and take the food elsewhere."

This reply drove Tortoise into a rage. He lifted up a stick that was lying nearby and he brought this down heavily on his mother's head. She died.

Snail helped him carry the body of his mother to her grave. Then, standing before the grave, Tortoise began to pray. No money came. Tortoise looked at Snail. Snail laughed.

11

An Old Man Who Saved Some Ungrateful People

In a certain village there lived people who were both happy and rich. They had very good fields there, and each year they harvested so much grain that their grain bins were full to overflowing. Some of the grain bins were so full, in fact, that the tree trunks which served as their legs broke and tipped the bins to the ground. This did not matter, as there was far more grain than was needed.

The birds heard about this village and decided that it would be a good place for birds to live. They arrived one morning, in a great fluttering cloud, and settled themselves on trees around the fields. Then, when the people had finished their work in the fields, the birds flew down and ate as much grain as they could manage. Then they flew back to their places in the trees and slept until the next morning.

The people were worried when they saw the next morning how much of the grain had been eaten by these

greedy birds. They shouted at the trees and shook their fists, but the birds just sang and paid no attention to the people below them.

The people returned to the village and got out all their bows and arrows. Then they walked back to the fields and aimed the arrows at the birds.

It was easy for the birds to avoid the arrows. As they saw them coming through the air, they just flew up until the arrows had passed. Then they landed on their branches again and began to sing.

"We shall soon starve," the women said to the headman. "If you do nothing, all the people in this village will stop being fat and will become very thin."

The headman knew that what they said was right. And yet he could think of no way in which they could deal with the birds. If their arrows did not work, then there was no other weapon at their disposal.

They talked and talked about the problem until one of the young men said:

"There is always that old man – the one we all chased away from the village. He knows many magic things and may be able to do something about the birds."

Everybody was silent. They had all been thinking the same thing but nobody had been courageous enough to talk about it. The old man had been chased away because of his spells and now they were going to have to beg him to come back again.

"Where does he live now?" asked the headman. "I think we shall have to go and speak to him."

The young man explained that he had seen the old man living in a bush not far away. He would be able to take the headman there and show him the place.

When the headman arrived at the bush in which the old man lived, he was saddened to see him in such a state. All his clothes were now rags and his cheeks were hollow. There were few leaves left on the bush, as the old man had been forced to eat leaves to deal with the great hunger which plagued him.

The headman greeted the old man and said how sorry he was that he had not seen him for such a long time. The old man looked at him, but said nothing.

"We are having a problem with birds," the head man then said. "Although we have good crops, the birds come down from the trees and eat all our grain. Soon we will be as poor as you are."

"You should shoot the birds," the old man said. "That's how you solve that problem."

"These birds are too clever," the headman said. "When our arrows come close to them, they hop up in the air and are unharmed."

The old man thought for a moment before he spoke again.

"I cannot help you," he said. "You made me leave that place before, and now I'm living in this new place."

The headman had feared that the old man would say something like this. He begged him to think again, and when the old man still said no, he begged him again. At last the old man agreed to come, although he was unhappy to leave the bush in which he was living.

Before they returned to the village, the old man went to a number of secret places which he knew and collected roots and other substances that he would need for his work. Then they went back to the village, where all the people were waiting to welcome the old man back into their midst.

* * *

The next morning, the old man called everybody in the village to the door of his hut. From a pouch which he had with him, he took out powders which he had made from roots and other substances. Everybody was then told to dip the tips of their arrows into this powder and, when they had done this, to go down to the fields and wait for him to come.

The birds watched the people gathering at the edge of the fields and laughed among themselves. The leader of the birds fluffed up his feathers and began to sing a special bird song which was all about how birds enjoyed eating the food of foolish people. Just as he sang, the old man took an arrow from a young man's bow and shot it towards the singing bird. The bird rose into the air, laughing at the useless weapons of the people below, but the arrow followed him upwards and pierced the centre of his heart.

89

All the other birds were silent when they saw what had happened to their leader. Before they could rise from their branches, though, many other arrows came up through the air and struck them down. After a few minutes, there were very few birds left, and these few took wing for the hills.

The village people were so happy at the fact that they had been saved that they took the old man to the largest hut they had and made him their new chief. They gave him four cows and a great supply of beer. Whenever he needed anything, he had only to ask, and it would be delivered to him.

The old man was happy to be a chief, and he ruled well. He never made unfair decisions, and he never took more than his fair share of anything. When people were squabbling over some little matter, he would settle the argument wisely. Everybody was content at the way he ruled.

After a while, some people began to talk about how the old man must still have powers to work magic.

"If he did it before," they said, "then he might do it again. He knows how these powders work."

Other people agreed.

"Perhaps one day he might use his magic against us,"

one man said. "If he did that, we would be powerless to stop him."

"We would be like the birds," another said. "He could shoot an arrow into our heart."

Such talk was soon going all around the village. Eventually, when enough people had heard it, they gathered in a crowd outside the old man's hut and shouted out for him to leave. The old man looked out of his door and was surprised to see the people standing there.

"I have done no wrong," he said. "Why are you asking me to leave?"

"Because you are too clever," the people said. "We are frightened of you."

The old man went back into his hut but soon came out again. Carrying the pouch with his powders in it, he left the village and returned to the bush where he had been living before he became chief. Satisfied with their work, the people had a party the next day to celebrate the departure of the old man. They did not see the birds sitting on the branches, watching the party.

* * *

When the people saw that the birds had returned, they began to wail.

"We shall have to find the old man again," they said. "We must bring him back to the village or we shall again lose all our crops."

As the birds descended on the fields and began to eat the grain, four of the most important men from the village ran off to find the old man. It took them some time to find him, but at last they reached the bush where he lived.

"You must come back to the village," they said. "We shall give you back your hut and your cows. You must come back."

The old man looked at the ungrateful people who stood before him. Then he looked at the bush, with its few leaves and the hard ground around it.

"No," he said.

13
Great Snake

When the chief called Mikizi died there was much discussion as to who should be the next chief. Mikizi had a son, but the mother of that boy did not want her son to be chief.

"He will never have any peace if he is a chief," she said. "Every day there will be people asking him to do things. This is a boy who likes to sleep. If he becomes a chief, he will never be able to sit on his stool and sleep all day."

The elders all knew that there was no point in trying to make that boy a chief and so they called all the witchdoctors in those parts to come to a meeting to help in the finding of a new chief. The leader of these witchdoctors said that there was only one way to find a new chief and that this was the way they should use.

"There is a hill near here," he said. "In the rocks around that hill there is a very large snake. Whoever can capture that great snake and bring it back here shall be made into the new chief."

The elders agreed that this was a very good way of choosing a new chief, although they doubted if anybody would be brave enough to try to capture that great snake. When a short boy came forward and said that he wished to try, they all laughed.

"Don't be so stupid," they said to him. "Short boys can never catch such large snakes."

"I should like to try," insisted the boy.

The elders said that he could not try but the boy kept asking again and again for their permission. At last they had had enough of his pestering and told him that he would be allowed to try.

"The snake will kill you," they warned him. "As you go down its throat, you should remember these words of ours."

* * *

The short boy set off towards the hill where the great snake lived. As he left the village, he heard people crying, and he knew that these were his friends who thought that he would never return. He paid no attention to their sorrow, though, as he knew that he would be able to capture the snake and bring it back to the village.

When he reached the first rocks that lay littered about the bottom of the hill, he stopped and listened to the sounds which were carried on the wind. He heard the swishing of the dry grass and the movement of the leaves in the trees. He heard the faint trickle of water and the sound of an eagle hunting high above the ground. And then he heard something else – the sound of a snake hissing.

The boy walked on until he was standing at the bottom of the hill. The sound he had heard was now quite loud and before much time had passed he saw the head of the great snake appear from a crack in the

rocks. The snake looked angry that a short boy should have come to disturb him, and with a sudden sliding it shot out and darted towards the boy's feet.

When he saw the snake coming towards him, the boy turned round and began to run away from the hill. He ran as fast as he could, but the snake just laughed at those short legs and drew closer and closer to the fleeing boy.

Looking over his shoulder, the short boy saw where the snake was and heard its laughter. He continued to run, but as he did so he took from his shoulder a calabash that he had hung there and began to drop things from it. First he dropped a lizard and then he dropped some frogs. After that he dropped some other small insects.

The snake came to the lizard and stopped. For a moment it seemed uncertain whether to carry on after the short boy, but then it opened its great mouth and swallowed the lizard. After it had done this, it resumed its chase of the boy, only to stop again when it came to the frogs jumping about on the ground.

The snake gobbled up the frogs, although it took it some time to catch them all. Then, its belly heavy with food, it slid on after the boy, only to stop again when it came to the insects.

By the time that the snake had eaten all the things that the boy dropped from the calabash, they were just outside the village fence. The boy called out to the elders that he was back and walked slowly through the gap in the fence.

"So," called out one of the elders. "You are back. Where is the great snake?"

The boy said nothing at first, then, with all the eyes of the village upon him, he turned round and pointed to the gate. As he did so, the great snake, fat and slow from all its eating, slid heavily into the village.

The people let out a great sigh when they saw the snake arrive and immediately the young men pinned it to the ground with sticks. The short boy stood before the elders and asked them if he could now be made the chief. The elders were surprised that such a short boy could be so brave but they remembered their promise and agreed to make him chief.

Later, when he was chief, the short boy grew taller.

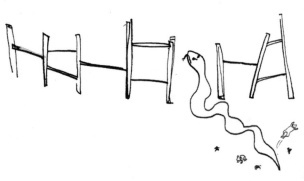

14
The Girl Who Married A Lion

Nearly everybody was happy when Kumalo's daughter married. Kumalo was pleased with the many fine cattle which his new son-in-law had given him; his wife was happy that she would no longer have to worry about what sort of man her daughter would marry; and the daughter herself was pleased that she had found such a fine, strong husband.

Only the new wife's brother was unhappy.

"I think that my sister has married a lion," he said to his friends. "This is really a lion disguised as a man."

Nobody took this seriously and they laughed at the young man when he said such things. But the brother knew that what he said was true, and he could not bring himself to talk to this new brother-in-law of his.

"I cannot talk to a lion," he said.

Several years passed and the wife had two strong sons, who were as handsome as their father. Still the wife's brother muttered that the husband was a lion

disguised as a man and still he refused to do anything with his brother-in-law.

"You're being stupid," Kumalo said. "Look at all the cattle that my daughter's husband gave me when he married her. Where would a lion get such cattle?"

The young man could not think of an answer to that question, but he refused to change his mind. He knew that sooner or later there would be trouble. And indeed one day his sister came to him and asked to talk to him in private.

"I am worried about this husband of mine," she whispered to her brother. "He has a strange smell on him."

"What sort of smell?" the brother asked.

The woman shrugged her shoulders. "It is a very strange smell," she said. "I cannot describe it."

In order to help his sister, the young man agreed to go to her hut and to smell some of the things that belonged to the husband. The husband was out at the time, and so it was easy for the wife to show the things that he carried with him. The brother smelled them and frowned.

"That is lion smell," he said.

The woman was very worried and she went with her brother to speak to their father. The old man was not happy to hear this news. He did not want to believe that his son-in-law was a lion, and so he said that they would test him to see if he really was a lion.

"We will put a goat outside his hut at night," he said. "If the goat is gone in the morning, then we will know that a lion has eaten it. That will prove that he is a lion."

Everyone agreed that this would be a good test and that night a goat was tethered outside the son-in-law's hut. The next morning, the father and the son went to the hut and saw that only the bones of the goat were left.

"No man would eat a goat like that," the son said triumphantly. "He is surely a lion."

The old man had to agree. It was hard to admit that such a thing had happened, but he had no other choice. There was only one thing to do: to fetch their spears

and to chase the son-in-law away from the home. The son-in-law was angry, of course, and tried to resist, but he could not fight the sharp points of the spears. As he ran off into the bush, both the father and his son saw that the marks where his feet had been were marks of a lion. This proved to them that they had been right. The woman was upset to have lost her fine husband, but she understood that it would have been impossible for her to continue to live with a lion. At any time her husband might have threatened to eat her.

Her brother thought that she would now be happy, but she came to see him again and it was clear that once again she was anxious.

"If my husband was a lion," she said to her brother, "then what are my two sons?"

The brother thought for a moment. He had not considered this problem and it made him worried. He loved his two nephews and it would be a sad blow if they turned out to be lions when they grew up. He looked closely at the two boys, but there were no signs that they were lions.

"We must be quite sure about this," he said to his sister. "We will have to test the boys in a special way."

Making a cage out of thin trees, the brother carried this to a lonely place where lions liked to walk. He put

the cage on the ground
and went back to fetch
the two boys. Then he
took them to the cage and told them to
get into it and sit there.

"I am testing this cage," he
explained to the boys. "I want
to see if it is strong enough to
give protection against lions.
I will come back tonight and
see if the lions have managed
to break into it."

The younger boy became very scared
of being left in the cage, but the elder one
comforted him.

"Our uncle would not put us in danger," he said.
"This cage must be strong enough to keep the lions
away."

The uncle had told his nephews that he was going
back to his hut, but in fact he hid in some trees nearby
and waited to see what happened. After a while, two
lions walked up to the cage and began to sniff at it.
The two boys cowered in the corner of the cage, and
the uncle could hear the younger one weeping.

After they had sniffed at the cage, the lions began
to roar. Then they started to dash at the cage, shaking

the thin wooden bars with their great weight. The two boys seemed very frightened and the uncle decided that if he did not go down to their rescue they would soon be eaten.

Leaping from his tree, the uncle rushed towards the lions, waving a long spear in his hand. The lions saw the spear and ran off into the bush, leaving the two frightened boys in the cage.

"Thank you, Uncle," the elder boy said. "I thought that we might be eaten by the lions."

The uncle smiled as he let his nephews out of the cage. Now he knew that they were not lions, for if they had been lions the real lions would have smelled it and would not have tried to attack them.

"Your sons are not lions," the uncle said to the boys' mother.

"I am glad," she said.

15
Greater
Than Lion

The hare did not like the lion. Every day the lion would walk about the bush, roaring. This frightened all the smaller animals, who feared that the lion would eat them. Even when the lion was not hungry he would roar, as if to say: "There is no greater animal than I. All animals should bow down before me."

It was true that there was no animal stronger than the lion, with the exception, perhaps, of the elephant. The elephant, though, was a shy creature. He disturbed nobody and would never walk round roaring. And if an elephant was ever attacked by a lion, there is no doubt that the elephant would retreat rather than stay and fight.

At last the hare decided that he must do something to stop the lion's constant bragging. He thought about it for over three days and just when he was about to admit that there was nothing that could be done, he had an idea. When the idea came to him he leapt up for the joy of it, just as hares are seen to leap in the early morning.

"Oh lion," he said to himself. "You will regret your boasts."

When the lion saw the hare coming towards him, he rose to his feet and let out a mighty roar. The hare felt the ground shake under him and he wondered whether he shouldn't run straight home. But he continued to approach the lion with the roars ringing in his ears like thunder.

"How dare you walk up to me like that," the lion shouted as the hare approached him. "Don't you know who I am? Don't you know that I'm the mightiest of beasts?"

The hare drew himself up to his full height and addressed the lion.

"Oh lion," he said. "I know that you are a mighty

beast. I know that all the animals in the bush are frightened of you."

The lion seemed pleased to hear this and dropped his voice a little.

"Well," he said. "At least you show me proper respect. But why have you come to see me?"

The hare looked carefully at the lion, knowing that what he was about to say was dangerous for him.

"I have come to tell you," he began, "that there is a creature who is greater than you."

When he heard these words, the lion roared again – a louder roar than the hare had ever heard. It seemed to him that the noise would knock him over and he cowered until the lion had stopped for breath.

"I don't mean to insult you," he said apologetically. "I just came to tell you."

The lion stared down at the small creature in front of him.

"Show me this animal," he said. "Let me see him."

The hare was relieved. "I can show you," he said. "But you will only be able to see him in a house."

"Then I shall go to this house," roared the lion. "Take me there right now."

The hare led the lion along the path to the house that he had specially prepared for him.

"You must go into that house," he said, pointing to the front door. "Then you will see the creature that is greater than you."

The lion bounded straight into the house and was quickly followed to the front door by the hare. Once the lion was safely inside, the hare bolted the front door and waited outside. Soon there came a thumping on the door as the lion realized that he was locked in.

"Where is this creature?" he shouted. "Fetch him at once."

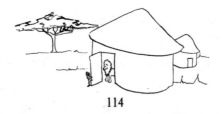

"Keep calm," called out the hare. "You'll see him soon. Just wait for him."

The lion went into the back room of the house and lay down on the cold stone floor. He waited all that day and all that night. The next morning the hare arrived at the front door and called out to the lion.

"Have you seen that creature yet?" he asked.

From within the house there came the sound of the lion's roar.

"No," he said. "I am the only creature here."

"He will come," promised the hare. "Just you wait."

The morning after that the hare returned at the same time and called out again to the lion.

"Is he there yet?" he asked.

This time the lion sounded angry. "No," he roared. "And let me out. I've had enough of this."

The hare ignored the lion's shouts and just laughed in reply.

"Just wait," he said. "Your visitor will come soon enough."

Many days passed before the hare came back again.

This time, when he called out, at first there came no reply from within the house.

"Lion," he called out. "Are you inside?"

After a few moments he heard a sound from the back room. It was not a great roar – it was more like the sound made by a tiny creature that lives among the leaves and twigs. Cautiously the hare opened the door and went into the house.

He found the lion lying on the floor of the back room. His tongue was out of his mouth, parched with thirst, and his ribs showed on his sides. He was so weak from the days without food and water that he was unable to raise his head to look at the hare. Only his eyes moved as the hare came up to him and peered into his face.

"I see that your visitor has come," the hare said. "The creature greater than you came after all."

The lion's eyes widened slightly.

"Who is he?" he asked in a tiny, weakened voice.

The hare laughed.

"Hunger," he replied.

16

Two Friends Who Met For Dinner

A man once asked a friend to have a meal with him. The friend was happy to receive this invitation, as he was never asked by anybody else to go anywhere. He spent a great deal of time making sure that he was smartly dressed for the meal so that his friend would be proud of him.

The guest arrived at his friend's house and was asked inside. Together they sat at the table and smelled the delicious smell of the food that had been cooked.

"All the food is in this calabash," said the host. "To get it out, you have to put your hand in the neck and take out a piece. I shall show you."

The host inserted his hand into the thin neck of the calabash and took out a morsel of food. It looked good, and the guest began to feel his mouth watering. Reaching across, he put his hand into the calabash and picked out a piece of food. Unfortunately, when he tried to take out his hand he found that it was too big to pass through the neck of the calabash with food in it. In order to get his hand out, he had to leave the food inside.

The host appeared not to notice the difficulty in which his guest found himself. He had small hands, and so he was able to take food out and put it into his mouth. He did not offer to give any food to his guest, although he handed him the calabash again and told him to help himself.

After a few minutes, the host had eaten all the food. He looked at his guest and smiled.

"I am sorry that you did not get much food," he said. "But if you have big hands, then that is one of the things that happens to you."

The guest said nothing. He was very sad that the only invitation that he had received for many years should have turned out to be such an unhappy occasion.

Some days later, the guest invited his host to dinner in his own hut. Before his friend arrived, however, he burned all the grass around his hut, so that the ground was black and charred with stubble.

The friend entered the hut and took off his hat.

"This is a good place," he said. "I am surprised that you do not have more friends, living in a comfortable place like this."

The other man smiled.

"The food is ready," he said. "But first, if you don't mind, you must wash your feet. People do not like dirty feet in this place."

The guest understood, and immediately walked off to the river to wash his feet. Then, when they were quite clean, he returned to the hut and found that the host had already started the meal. The host looked at the guest's feet and shook his head.

"I'm afraid that your feet are still very dirty," he said. "You will have to return to the river and wash them again. This is very good food here and I do not want it spoiled by dirty feet."

The guest knew that this was right, but he could not understand why his feet were so dirty after he had

washed them so carefully. This time, he ran to the river's edge and washed both feet thoroughly. Then, checking to see that they were quite clean, he ran back to the hut. On his way, of course, he passed through the middle of the charred stubble that surrounded his friend's hut. This soon covered his feet and made them dirty again.

"Oh dear," said the friend. "I must ask you to wash your feet one more time. Look at how dirty they are."

The friend was now becoming angry, but he ran back to the river and washed the dirty feet again. Then he returned to the hut.

The friend looked at him.

"I'm sorry," he said. "I have just finished all the good food I prepared for the meal. Also, I'm very sorry to tell you, your feet are still dirty."

17

Tremendously Clever Tricks Are Played, But To Limited Effect

There was a terrible drought once, with all the land crying out for water and the sky quite empty of clouds. The people stood and thought about rain, which they had almost forgotten, so long ago had the last rains fallen. And it was very bad for the animals too, who had to look in all sorts of places for water. They began to die, falling to the ground and staring up with lifeless eyes at the sky from which no water came.

Eventually the animals decided to hold a meeting. They all came together, walking slowly because of their thirst, and they talked to one another about what might be done.

"We must dig a well," said Hyena. "That is the way to get water when there is no rain."

Of course it is easy for people to dig a well, as they have hands that can work the earth. But for animals

it is a hard task, as they
must scrape at the soil
with their feet; it is slow, slow work
for them. But all the animals did
their part of the work – all except for Hare, who was
lazy. When asked why he was not helping to find water,
he replied that his family totem was water and therefore
he had no need to drink. "You must drink," he said, "but
I do not need to. I shall watch you work."

The animals were very fortunate in finding a good
supply of water under the ground. They all drank their
fill and then began to leave the well. When they returned,
though, they found that the water was dirtied – somebody had been drinking from it in their absence.

"We must leave somebody on guard," said Elephant.
"Then that animal will be able to stop the water from
being dirtied while we are off hunting."

It was agreed that Hyena would take on this task on the
first day, and he was duly left there, while all the others
went off in search of food. He sat in the shade of a tree
and thought about things that hyenas like to think about,
which are not things that you and I would understand.

After a short while he heard somebody coming. This person was singing, and it turned out to be Hare himself. "I am very happy," he sang. "Some boys have dug a well for me/ Now I can drink and wash in the water to my heart's content/ I am a happy hare."

Hyena was furious, and charged at Hare. Hare dodged his charge and then came towards him slowly, offering him a large piece of honeycomb. Hyena, who was greedy, took the honey and ate it all, while Hare sneaked off behind him and drank and washed in the water.

When Hyena saw that he had been tricked in this way, his heart burst within him, so great was his anger. Then he died.

When the animals came back, they were saddened to see that the water had been so dirtied. They found the body of their friend, Hyena, and many of the animals wept for him, as even an animal like Hyena is loved by some.

The next day Jackal offered to stay behind and guard the water. "I am a very cunning creature," he said. "Nobody will be able to trick me."

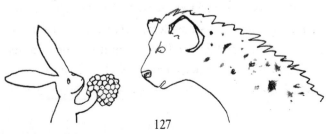

Hare came by again. This time he threw pieces of meat in front of Jackal, who ate them all up. The meat was delicious, and there was a great deal of it. As a result, Jackal became too fat to run after Hare as he went to the water and drank half of what was there and dirtied the rest.

On their return, the animal were furious with Jackal who had failed in his task all because of his greediness. They decided that the only thing to do was to kill him and to leave a girl in charge of the water.

"A girl will not be fooled so easily," thought the animals. "It is easy to fool animals, but a girl is different."

Once the animals had gone away again, Hare sauntered along and told the girl that if she tried to stop him he would punch her with his hare fists. The girl said that this would not worry her, and so Hare punched her with his right fist. This fist stuck to the girl, and so he punched her with his other fist, and again the same

thing happened. This left Hare with his head as the only weapon at his disposal. But his head stuck to the girl too, and it was at this point that the animals all came back and saw the wicked hare stuck to the girl. They decided that he must be killed for taking their water.

"The only way to kill a hare," said Hare, "is by hare tradition. This means that you will have to swing me round and round and then smash me to the ground. That is the way it must be done."

The animals agreed to this and Elephant, who was the strongest, was given the task of swinging Hare round and

round with his trunk. But as he did so, Hare slipped out of his skin and sailed away in the air. When he landed safely, he turned and laughed at the animals, saying that they were perfectly welcome to kill his skin if they wished. So he ran off, laughing, although he had no skin now.

Hare did not return. The girl who caught him was praised by all the animals, and was allowed to share their water. This made her happy too.